Dumpy's
Happy Holiday

Julie Andrews Edwards and Emma Walton Hamilton
Illustrated by Tony Walton

An early December sun touched the frosty holiday lights that had been twinkling all night in Apple Harbor.

The rooster on the old barn roof at Merryhill Farm fluffed his feathers and announced the morning to the world:

"COCK-A-DOODLE-DOO"

Up at the farmhouse, the Barnes family was enjoying Sunday breakfast.

"The newspaper says people are giving less to charity this year," Farmer Barnes noted.

"What's charity?" asked young Charlie.

"Charity means giving, pal," his grandfather Pop-Up explained. "Charities are organizations that help people who are less fortunate than we are."

"It seems children in Africa are especially in need of toys," added the farmer.

"Could *we* help?" asked Charlie. "What if everyone in our village gave a book or toy? We could use Dumpy to collect them!"

Mrs. Barnes smiled. "But where would we send it all?"

"These things have a way of working themselves out!" Pop-Up announced. "And remember, charity begins at home."

So the Barnes family set to work.

They painted big signs that read "APPLE HARBOR CHARITY DRIVE!" and "HELP A NEEDY CHILD THIS HOLIDAY!" They decorated Dumpy from fender to tailgate, and finished the job by placing a cardboard crown on his radiator cap.

Dumpy felt very important, and ready for business.

Every day after school, Pop-Up
and Charlie drove Dumpy slowly through
the village. "Bring a child some holiday joy!
Please donate a special toy!" they called.
Dumpy said, "TOOT! TOOT!" so loudly and so
often that people came out of their houses to see what the fuss was about.

Little by little, everyone began to contribute to the cause . . . and eventually, a wonderful array of goodies filled Dumpy's dumper. His tires began to sag from the weight of it all.

"So much for people giving less this year." Pop-Up grinned at Charlie. "I guess every charity could use a Dumpy!"

"But we still don't know where to send it all," Charlie worried. "The holidays are almost here! How will the children in Africa get the toys?"

"Details, details," said Pop-Up. "Remember, things have a way of working themselves out!"

Dumpy suddenly coughed, wheezed, and shuddered to a halt at the bottom of Merry Hill.

"That's not exactly what I had in mind . . ." said Pop-Up.

"Err-r-r! Err-r-! r r-r"

Dumpy protested as Pop-Up turned the key in his ignition.

"Did you remember to fill the gas tank this morning?" Charlie asked politely.

"Ahhh." Pop-Up held up his finger. "I wondered what this string was for."

Charlie pointed to a large house across the street.

"Miss Dominic might let us use her phone . . ." he began, but the stately dowager was already sailing down the path toward them, looking decidedly irritated.

"Parking at the bottom of this hill is *not* allowed," she announced.

"Deepest apologies, dear lady." Pop-Up bowed. "Our charity drive has come to a grinding halt."

"Good gracious!" Miss Dominic spotted Dumpy's cargo. "Where are you taking all this?"

"We don't know yet," replied Charlie, and explained about their delivery problem.

Miss Dominic's eyes sparkled. "I think I just might be able to help," she said.

A phone call and a gallon of gas later, Charlie and Pop-Up found themselves in the offices of *The Harbor Herald* newspaper. Miss Dominic stood before the hastily assembled staff and addressed them all.

"I never presume to tell you your business," she said. "But as owner of *The Herald*, I've seldom found a cause so worthy of our support. This will make a *great* news story . . . let's take it to the top!"

The next morning, Charlie, Pop-Up, and Farmer Barnes set off in Dumpy for the big city.

"What if there's nobody at the United Nations?" Charlie asked.

"Not likely, pal," Pop-Up reassured him. "Miss Dominic spoke to the boss personally. He's expecting us."

"The boss of the whole world?" Charlie gasped.

"Just of the United Nations." Pop-Up smiled. "He's called the Secretary General, and he helps keep the peace between countries."

"Too bad he can't keep the peace in this traffic," said Farmer Barnes wryly. Cars and trucks around them had slowed to a halt and were **HONK**ing angrily at each other.

"What if we're late?" Charlie worried.

"Things have a way . . ." said Pop-Up.

". . . of working themselves out." Charlie nodded.

"WEE-OO, WEE-OO, WEE!"

A familiar sound approached from behind. "When there's trouble, count on **MEE!**" Polly the Police Car came **ZOOM**ing down the shoulder of the road beside them.

"Hello, Barnes family!" Sergeant Molly Mott called. "Heard about the traffic on the two-way—thought Dumpy could use a police escort."

"*Awesome!*" gasped Charlie.

"The heart of Apple Harbor is in that dumper," Sergeant Mott shouted. "Gotta make our village proud. Follow me!" Red lights flashing, the police car took off.

"BROOOM! BROOOM!"

roared Dumpy, and peeled out behind her.

They bowled along the emergency lane, and perhaps because of the
holiday spirit and Dumpy's festive appearance, an encouraging cheer
went up as they passed all the stalled traffic.

Charlie bounced in his seat.
"This is SO COOL!" he kept saying.
The tollbooth man saluted and lifted his barrier as
Polly and Dumpy headed for a long tunnel. They came out
the other side, and suddenly the big city was all around them.

Towering skyscrapers gleamed in the sunlight. Holiday decorations, bigger than any in Apple Harbor, lit the busy streets and stores. Taxis **BEEP**ed a noisy accompaniment to Polly's siren as they *ZOOM*ed uptown. Dumpy was dizzy from the hustle and bustle of it all.

"'Atta boy, Dumpy!" Pop-Up was charged with excitement.

"Where is it? Where is it?" Charlie pressed.

"THERE!" Farmer Barnes pointed, and all at once they saw the United Nations building standing majestically at the edge of the river.

"Told you they'd be expecting us." Pop-Up grinned as security guards waved Polly and Dumpy past the barricades.

"But we still don't know how the gifts will get to Africa . . ." Charlie worried, then quickly added, "I know, I know. Things have a way . . ."

Dumpy pulled alongside the United Nations plaza and came to a breathless halt.

There was a momentary silence.

Then a wondrous sound filled the air: Dozens of children were gathered on the grounds, singing lustily.

A dignified gentleman approached Dumpy.

"Welcome to the United Nations!" he said. "I am the Secretary General, and you have come on a special day. The African Children's Choir is giving a holiday concert!" Dumpy's engine suddenly PINGed, and Charlie gasped as an idea struck him.

"Would they take our gifts to the children who need them?" he asked.
"I think they'd be delighted," said the Secretary General with a smile.

The children gathered around and unloaded Dumpy's cargo as a swarm of photographers descended. Amidst a sea of faces and flashing lights, Charlie and Pop-Up grinned at each other.

"Didn't I say things have a way of working themselves out?" Pop-Up winked.

At breakfast the next morning, Farmer Barnes unfolded his newspaper with a flourish.

There was Dumpy on the front page, under a huge headline: **"DUMPY'S HAPPY HOLIDAY."**

"Things *did* work out—thanks to Dumpy," said Charlie proudly. "Let's deliver apples and Merryhill maple syrup to everyone in the village next!"

"Charity *rules*!" Pop-Up gave him a hug. "We'll start right after breakfast."

And that's exactly what they did!

For Hope and Hank — and Zöe, of course . . .
with all our love!

Dumpy's Happy Holiday • Text copyright © 2004 by Dumpy, LLC • Illustrations copyright © 2004 by Tony Walton
Manufactured in China. • All rights reserved. • www.harperchildrens.com
Library of Congress Cataloging-in-Publication Data • Edwards, Julie, date. • Dumpy's happy holiday / Julie Andrews Edwards
and Emma Walton Hamilton ; illustrated by Tony Walton.—1st ed. • p.   cm.—(The Julie Andrews collection) • Summary: When
Farmer Barnes tells his family that people are giving less to charity, and children in Africa need toys, they decorate Dumpy the Dumptruck
and set off on the Apple Harbor Charity Drive. • ISBN 0-06-052684-X — ISBN 0-06-052685-8 (lib. bdg.) • [1. Charity—Fiction.
2. Christmas—Fiction. 3. Dump trucks—Fiction. 4. Trucks—Fiction.] I. Hamilton, Emma Walton. II. Walton, Tony, ill. III. Title.
IV. Series. • PZ7.E2562 Dx 2004 • [E]—dc21 • 2003006230 • CIP • AC
Typography by Amelia M. Anderson • 1 2 3 4 5 6 7 8 9 10 • ❖ • First Edition

Color preparation by Cassandra Boyd